RABINDRANATH TAGORE

Born in Calcutta (now Kolkata) in 1861, Rabindranath Tagore was an innovative polymath who reshaped Bengali literature and music. In 1913 he became Asia's first Nobel Prize winner for his famous volume of verse and lyrics published as *Gitanjali.*

Tagore's creative output was staggering, encompassing thousands of songs as well as novels, lyrics and poems, plays, personal and political essays and paintings. However, it was through his short stories that he reshaped Bengali literature, introducing a less formal style whose freshness and psychological depth was so different from traditional classical writing. With his elegant and charming prose, he captured the ordinary lives of both rural and urban dwellers whilst encompassing universal themes such as love, loyalty and hope. Tagore, who died in 1941, is remembered as India's most famous modern poet.

RABINDRANATH TAGORE

The Home-Coming

'The Home-Coming' first published 1892
'The Cabuliwallah' first published 1892
'Mashi' first published 1918
'The Skeleton' first published 1892
'The Postmaster' first published 1891

This edition first published 2026 by Macmillan Collector's Library
an imprint of Pan Macmillan
The Smithson, 6 Briset Street, London EC1M 5NR
EU representative: Macmillan Publishers Ireland Ltd, 1st Floor,
The Liffey Trust Centre, 117–126 Sheriff Street Upper,
Dublin 1 D01 YC43
Associated companies throughout the world

ISBN 978-1-0374-0343-9

1 3 5 7 9 8 6 4 2

A CIP catalogue record for this book is available from the British Library.

Cover design: Tiana-Jane Dunlop, Pan Macmillan Art Department
Typeset in Adobe Caslon Pro by Six Red Marbles UK, Thetford, Norfolk
Printed and bound in the UK using 100% Renewable Electricity by CPI Group (UK) Ltd

CONTENTS

The Home-Coming

Phatik Chakravorti was ringleader among the boys of the village. A new mischief got into his head. There was a heavy log lying on the mud-flat of the river waiting to be shaped into a mast for a boat. He decided that they should all work together to shift the log by main force from its place and roll it away. The owner of the log would be angry and surprised, and they would all enjoy the fun. Every one seconded the proposal, and it was carried unanimously.

But just as the fun was about to begin, Mākhan, Phatik's younger brother, sauntered up, and sat down on the log in front of them all without a word. The boys were puzzled for a moment. He was pushed, rather timidly, by one of the boys and told to get up: but he remained quite unconcerned. He appeared like a young philosopher meditating on the futility of games. Phatik was furious. "Mākhan," he cried, "if you don't get down this minute, I'll thrash you!"

Mākhan only moved to a more comfortable position.

Now, if Phatik was to keep his regal dignity before the public, it was clear he ought to carry out his threat. But his courage failed him at the crisis. His fertile brain, however, rapidly seized upon a new manœuvre which would discomfit his brother and afford his followers an added amusement. He gave the word of command to roll the log and Mākhan over together. Mākhan heard the order, and made it a point of honour to stick on. But he overlooked the fact, like those who attempt earthly fame in other matters, that there was peril in it.

The boys began to heave at the log with all their might, calling out, "One, two, three, go." At the word "go" the log went; and with it went Mākhan's philosophy, glory and all.

All the other boys shouted themselves hoarse with delight. But Phatik was a little frightened. He knew what was coming. And, sure enough, Mākhan rose from Mother Earth blind as Fate and screaming like the Furies. He rushed at Phatik and scratched his face and beat him and kicked him, and then went crying home. The first act of the drama was over.

Phatik wiped his face, and sat down on the edge of a sunken barge on the river bank, and began to chew a piece of grass. A boat came up to the landing, and a middle-aged man, with grey hair and dark moustache, stepped on shore. He saw the boy sitting there doing nothing, and asked him where the Chakravortis lived. Phatik went on chewing the grass, and said: "Over there," but it was quite impossible to tell where he pointed. The stranger asked him again. He swung his legs to and fro on the side of the barge, and said:

"Go and find out," and continued to chew the grass as before.

But now a servant came down from the house, and told Phatik his mother wanted him. Phatik refused to move. But the servant was the master on this occasion. He took Phatik up roughly, and carried him, kicking and struggling in impotent rage.

When Phatik came into the house, his mother saw him. She called out angrily: "So you have been hitting Mākhan again?"

Phatik answered indignantly: "No, I haven't; who told you that?"

His mother shouted: "Don't tell lies! You have."

Phatik said suddenly: "I tell you, I haven't. You ask Mākhan!" But Mākhan thought it best to stick to his previous statement. He said: "Yes, mother. Phatik did hit me."

Phatik's patience was already exhausted. He could not bear this injustice. He rushed at Mākhan, and hammered him with blows: "Take that," he cried, "and that, and that, for telling lies."

His mother took Mākhan's side in a moment, and pulled Phatik away, beating him with her hands. When Phatik pushed her aside, she shouted out: "What! you little villain! would you hit your own mother?"

It was just at this critical juncture that the grey-haired stranger arrived. He asked what was the matter. Phatik looked sheepish and ashamed.

But when his mother stepped back and looked at the stranger, her anger was changed to surprise. For she recognised her brother, and cried: "Why, Dada! Where have you come from?"

As she said these words, she bowed to the ground and touched his feet. Her brother had gone away soon after she had married, and he had started business in Bombay. His sister had lost her husband while he was in Bombay. Bishamber had now come back to Calcutta, and had at once made enquiries about his sister. He had then hastened to see her as soon as he found out where she was.

The next few days were full of rejoicing. The brother asked after the education of the two boys. He was told by his sister that Phatik was a perpetual nuisance. He was lazy, disobedient, and wild. But Mākhan was as good as gold, as quiet as a lamb, and very fond of reading. Bishamber kindly offered to take Phatik off his sister's hands, and educate him with his own children in Calcutta. The widowed mother readily agreed. When his uncle asked Phatik if he would like to go to Calcutta with him, his joy knew no bounds, and he said: "Oh, yes, uncle!" in a way that made it quite clear that he meant it.

It was an immense relief to the mother to get rid of Phatik. She had a prejudice against the boy, and no love was lost between the two brothers. She was in daily fear that he would either drown Mākhan some day in the river, or break his head in a fight, or run him into some danger or other. At the same time she was somewhat distressed to see Phatik's extreme eagerness to get away.

Phatik, as soon as all was settled, kept asking his uncle every minute when they were to start. He was on pins and needles all day long with excitement, and lay awake most of the night. He bequeathed to Mākhan, in perpetuity, his fishing-rod, his big kite and his marbles. Indeed, at this time of departure his generosity towards Mākhan was unbounded.

When they reached Calcutta, Phatik made the acquaintance of his aunt for the first time. She was by no means pleased with this unnecessary addition to her family. She found her own three boys quite enough to manage without taking any one else. And to bring a village lad of fourteen into their midst was terribly upsetting. Bishamber should really have thought twice before committing such an indiscretion.

In this world of human affairs there is no worse nuisance than a boy at the age of fourteen. He is neither ornamental, nor useful. It is impossible to shower affection on him as on a little boy; and he is always getting in the way. If he talks with a childish lisp he is called a baby, and if he answers in a grown-up way he is called impertinent. In fact any talk at all from him is resented. Then he is at the unattractive, growing age. He grows out of his clothes with indecent haste; his voice grows hoarse and breaks and quavers; his face grows suddenly angular and unsightly. It is easy to excuse the shortcomings of early childhood, but it is hard to tolerate even unavoidable lapses in a boy of fourteen. The lad himself becomes painfully self-conscious. When he talks with elderly people he is either unduly forward, or else so unduly shy that he appears ashamed of his very existence.

Yet it is at this very age when in his heart of hearts a young lad most craves for recognition and love; and he becomes the devoted slave of any one who shows him consideration. But none dare openly love him, for that would be regarded as undue indulgence, and therefore bad for the boy. So, what with scolding and chiding, he becomes very much like a stray dog that has lost his master.

For a boy of fourteen his own home is the only Paradise. To live in a strange house with strange people is little short of torture, while the height of bliss is to receive the kind looks of women, and never to be slighted by them.

It was anguish to Phatik to be the unwelcome guest in his aunt's house, despised by this elderly woman, and slighted on every occasion. If she ever asked him to do anything for her, he would be so overjoyed that he would overdo it; and then she would tell him not to be so stupid, but to get on with his lessons.

The cramped atmosphere of neglect in his aunt's house oppressed Phatik so much that he felt that he could hardly breathe. He wanted to go out into the open country and fill his lungs and breathe freely. But there was no open country to go to. Surrounded on all sides by Calcutta houses and walls, he would dream night after night of his village home, and long to be back there. He remembered the glorious meadow where he used to fly his kite all day long; the broad river-banks where he would wander about the livelong day singing and shouting for joy; the narrow brook where he could go and dive and swim at any time he liked. He thought of his band of boy companions over whom he was despot; and, above all, the memory of that tyrant mother of his, who had such a prejudice against him, occupied him day and night. A kind of physical love like that of animals; a longing to be in the presence of the one who is loved; an inexpressible wistfulness during absence; a silent cry of the inmost heart for the mother, like the lowing of a calf in the twilight;—this love, which was almost an animal instinct, agitated the shy, nervous, lean, uncouth and ugly boy. No one could understand it, but it preyed upon his mind continually.

There was no more backward boy in the whole school than Phatik. He gaped and remained silent when the teacher asked him a question, and like an overladen ass patiently suffered all the blows that came down on his back. When other boys were out at play, he stood wistfully by the window and gazed at the roofs of the distant houses. And if by chance he espied children playing on the open terrace of any roof, his heart would ache with longing.

One day he summoned up all his courage, and asked his uncle: "Uncle, when can I go home?"

His uncle answered: "Wait till the holidays come."

But the holidays would not come till November, and there was a long time still to wait.

One day Phatik lost his lesson-book. Even with the help of books he had found it very difficult indeed to prepare his lesson. Now it was impossible. Day after day the teacher would cane him unmercifully. His condition became so abjectly miserable that even his cousins were ashamed to own him. They began to jeer and insult him more than the other boys. He went to his aunt at last, and told her that he had lost his book.

His aunt pursed her lips in contempt, and said: "You great clumsy, country lout. How can I afford, with all my family, to buy you new books five times a month?"

That night, on his way back from school, Phatik had a bad headache with a fit of shivering. He felt he was going to have an attack of malarial fever. His one great fear was that he would be a nuisance to his aunt.

The next morning Phatik was nowhere to be seen. All searches in the neighbourhood proved futile. The rain had been pouring in torrents all night, and those who went out in search of the boy got drenched through to the skin. At last Bishamber asked help from the police.

At the end of the day a police van stopped at the door before the house. It was still raining and the streets were all flooded. Two constables brought out Phatik in their arms and placed him before Bishamber. He was wet through from head to foot, muddy all over, his face and eyes flushed red with fever, and his limbs all trembling. Bishamber carried him in his arms, and took him into the inner apartments. When his wife saw him, she exclaimed: "What a heap of trouble this boy has given us. Hadn't you better send him home?"

Phatik heard her words, and sobbed out loud: "Uncle, I was just going home; but they dragged me back again."

The fever rose very high, and all that night the boy was delirious. Bishamber brought in a doctor. Phatik opened his eyes flushed with fever, and looked up to the ceiling, and said vacantly: "Uncle, have the holidays come yet? May I go home?"

Bishamber wiped the tears from his own eyes, and took Phatik's lean and burning hands in his own, and sat by him through the night. The boy began again to mutter. At last his voice became excited: "Mother," he cried, "don't beat me like that! Mother! I am telling the truth!"

The next day Phatik became conscious for a short time. He turned his eyes about the room, as if expecting some one to come. At last, with an air of disappointment, his head sank back on the pillow. He turned his face to the wall with a deep sigh.

Bishamber knew his thoughts, and, bending down his head, whispered: "Phatik, I have sent for your mother."

The day went by. The doctor said in a troubled voice that the boy's condition was very critical.

Phatik began to cry out: "By the mark!—three fathoms. By the mark—four fathoms. By the mark——." He had heard the sailor on the river-steamer calling out the mark on the plumb-line. Now he was himself plumbing an unfathomable sea.

Later in the day Phatik's mother burst into the room like a whirlwind, and began to toss from side to side and moan and cry in a loud voice.

Bishamber tried to calm her agitation, but she flung herself on the bed, and cried: "Phatik, my darling, my darling."

Phatik stopped his restless movements for a moment. His hands ceased beating up and down. He said: "Eh?"

The mother cried again: "Phatik, my darling, my darling."

Phatik very slowly turned his head and, without seeing anybody, said: "Mother, the holidays have come."

The Cabuliwallah

My five years' old daughter Mini cannot live without chattering. I really believe that in all her life she has not wasted a minute in silence. Her mother is often vexed at this, and would stop her prattle, but I would not. To see Mini quiet is unnatural, and I cannot bear it long. And so my own talk with her is always lively.

One morning, for instance, when I was in the midst of the seventeenth chapter of my new novel, my little Mini stole into the room, and putting her hand into mine, said: "Father! Ramdayal the door-keeper calls a crow a krow! He doesn't know anything, does he?"

Before I could explain to her the differences of language in this world, she was embarked on the full tide of another subject. "What do you think, Father? Bhola says there is an elephant in the clouds, blowing water out of his trunk, and that is why it rains!"

And then, darting off anew, while I sat still making ready some reply to this last saying, "Father! what relation is Mother to you?"

"My dear little sister in the law!" I murmured

involuntarily to myself, but with a grave face contrived to answer: "Go and play with Bhola, Mini! I am busy!"

The window of my room overlooks the road. The child had seated herself at my feet near my table, and was playing softly, drumming on her knees. I was hard at work on my seventeenth chapter, where Protrap Singh, the hero, had just caught Kanchanlata, the heroine, in his arms, and was about to escape with her by the third story window of the castle, when all of a sudden Mini left her play, and ran to the window, crying, "A Cabuliwallah! a Cabuliwallah!" Sure enough in the street below was a Cabuliwallah, passing slowly along. He wore the loose soiled clothing of his people, with a tall turban; there was a bag on his back, and he carried boxes of grapes in his hand.

I cannot tell what were my daughter's feelings at the sight of this man, but she began to call him loudly. "Ah!" I thought, "he will come in, and my seventeenth chapter will never be finished!" At which exact moment the Cabuliwallah turned, and looked up at the child. When she saw this, overcome by terror, she fled to her mother's protection, and disappeared. She had a blind belief that inside the bag, which the big man carried, there were perhaps two or three other children like herself. The pedlar meanwhile entered my doorway, and greeted me with a smiling face.

So precarious was the position of my hero and my heroine, that my first impulse was to stop and buy something, since the man had been called. I made some small purchases, and a conversation began about Abdurrahman, the Russians, the English, and the Frontier Policy.

As he was about to leave, he asked: "And where is the little girl, sir?"

And I, thinking that Mini must get rid of her false fear, had her brought out.

She stood by my chair, and looked at the Cabuliwallah and his bag. He offered her nuts and raisins, but she would not be tempted, and only clung the closer to me, with all her doubts increased.

This was their first meeting.

One morning, however, not many days later, as I was leaving the house, I was startled to find Mini, seated on a bench near the door, laughing and talking, with the great Cabuliwallah at her feet. In all her life, it appeared, my small daughter had never found so patient a listener, save her father. And already the corner of her little *sari* was stuffed with almonds and raisins, the gift of her visitor. "Why did you give her those?" I said, and taking out an eight-anna bit, I handed it to him. The man accepted the money without demur, and slipped it into his pocket.

Alas, on my return an hour later, I found the unfortunate coin had made twice its own worth of trouble! For the Cabuliwallah had given it to Mini, and her mother catching sight of the bright round object, had pounced on the child with: "Where did you get that eight-anna bit?"

"The Cabuliwallah gave it me," said Mini cheerfully.

"The Cabuliwallah gave it you!" cried her mother much shocked. "Oh, Mini! how could you take it from him?"

I, entering at the moment, saved her from impending disaster, and proceeded to make my own inquiries.

It was not the first or second time, I found, that the two had met. The Cabuliwallah had overcome the child's first terror by a judicious bribery of nuts and almonds, and the two were now great friends.

They had many quaint jokes, which afforded them much amusement. Seated in front of him, looking down on his gigantic frame in all her tiny dignity, Mini would ripple her face with laughter, and begin: "O Cabuliwallah, Cabuliwallah, what have you got in your bag?"

And he would reply, in the nasal accents of the mountaineer: "An elephant!" Not much cause for merriment, perhaps; but how they both enjoyed the witticism! And for me, this child's talk with a grown-up man had always in it something strangely fascinating.

Then the Cabuliwallah, not to be behindhand, would take his turn: "Well, little one, and when are you going to the father-in-law's house?"

Now most small Bengali maidens have heard long ago about the father-in-law's house; but we, being a little new-fangled, had kept these things from our child, and Mini at this question must have been a trifle bewildered. But she would not show it, and with ready tact replied: "Are *you* going there?"

Amongst men of the Cabuliwallah's class, however, it is well known that the words *father-in-law's house* have a double meaning. It is a euphemism for *jail,* the place where we are well cared for, at no expense to ourselves. In this sense would the sturdy pedlar take my daughter's question. "Ah," he would say, shaking his fist at an invisible policeman, "I will thrash my father-in-law!" Hearing this, and picturing the poor discomfited relative, Mini would go off into peals of laughter, in which her formidable friend would join.

These were autumn mornings, the very time of year when kings of old went forth to conquest; and I, never stirring from my little corner in Calcutta, would let my mind wander over the whole world. At the very name of another country, my heart would go out to it, and at the sight of a foreigner in the streets, I would fall to weaving a network of dreams,—the mountains, the glens, and the forests of his distant home, with his cottage in its setting, and the free and independent life of far-away wilds. Perhaps the scenes of travel conjure themselves up before me, and pass and repass in my imagination all the more vividly, because I lead such a vegetable existence, that a call to travel would fall upon me like a thunderbolt. In the presence of this Cabuliwallah, I was immediately transported to the foot of arid mountain peaks, with narrow little defiles twisting in and out amongst their towering heights. I could see the string of camels bearing the merchandise, and the company of turbaned merchants, carrying some of their queer old firearms, and some of their spears, journeying downward towards the plains. I could see—but at some such point Mini's mother would intervene, imploring me to "beware of that man."

Mini's mother is unfortunately a very timid lady. Whenever she hears a noise in the street, or sees people coming towards the house, she always jumps to the conclusion that they are either thieves, or drunkards, or snakes, or tigers, or malaria or cockroaches, or caterpillars, or an English sailor. Even after all these years of experience, she is not able to overcome her terror. So she was full of doubts about the Cabuliwallah, and used to beg me to keep a watchful eye on him.

I tried to laugh her fear gently away, but then she would turn round on me seriously, and ask me solemn questions.

Were children never kidnapped?

Was it, then, not true that there was slavery in Cabul?

Was it so very absurd that this big man should be able to carry off a tiny child?

I urged that, though not impossible, it was highly improbable. But this was not enough, and her dread persisted. As it was indefinite, however, it did not seem right to forbid the man the house, and the intimacy went on unchecked.

Once a year in the middle of January Rahmun, the Cabuliwallah, was in the habit of returning to his country, and as the time approached he would be very busy, going from house to house collecting his debts. This year, however, he could always find time to come and see Mini. It would have seemed to an outsider that there was some conspiracy between the two, for when he could not come in the morning, he would appear in the evening.

Even to me it was a little startling now and then, in the corner of a dark room, suddenly to surprise this tall, loose-garmented, much bebagged man; but when Mini would run in smiling, with her, "O! Cabuliwallah! Cabuliwallah!" and the two friends, so far apart in age, would subside into their old laughter and their old jokes, I felt reassured.

One morning, a few days before he had made up his mind to go, I was correcting my proof sheets in my study. It was chilly weather. Through the window the rays of the sun touched my feet, and the slight warmth was very welcome. It was almost eight o'clock, and the early pedestrians were returning home, with their heads covered. All at once, I heard an uproar in the street, and, looking out, saw Rahmun being led away bound between two policemen, and behind them a crowd of curious boys. There were blood-stains on the clothes of the Cabuliwallah, and one of the policemen carried a knife. Hurrying out, I stopped them, and enquired what it all meant. Partly from one, partly from another, I gathered that a certain neighbour had owed the pedlar something for a Rampuri shawl, but had falsely denied having bought it, and that in the course of the quarrel, Rahmun had struck him. Now in the heat of his excitement, the prisoner began calling his enemy all sorts of names, when suddenly in a verandah of my house appeared my little Mini, with her usual exclamation: "O Cabuliwallah! Cabuliwallah!" Rahmun's face lighted up as he turned to her. He had no bag under his arm to-day, so she could not discuss the elephant with him. She at once therefore proceeded to the next question: "Are you going to the father-in-law's house?" Rahmun laughed and said: "Just where I am going, little one!" Then seeing that the reply did not amuse the child, he held up his fettered hands. "Ah," he said, "I would have thrashed that old father-in-law, but my hands are bound!"

On a charge of murderous assault, Rahmun was sentenced to some years' imprisonment.

Time passed away, and he was not remembered. The accustomed work in the accustomed place was ours, and the thought of the once-free mountaineer spending his years in prison seldom or never occurred to us. Even my light-hearted Mini, I am ashamed to say, forgot her old friend. New companions filled her life. As she grew older, she spent more of her time with girls. So much time indeed did she spend with them that she came no more, as she used to do, to her father's room. I was scarcely on speaking terms with her.

Years had passed away. It was once more autumn and we had made arrangements for our Mini's marriage. It was to take place during the Puja Holidays. With Durga returning to Kailas, the light of our home also was to depart to her husband's house, and leave her father's in the shadow.

The morning was bright. After the rains, there was a sense of ablution in the air, and the sun-rays looked like pure gold. So bright were they that they gave a beautiful radiance even to the sordid brick walls of our Calcutta lanes. Since early dawn to-day the wedding-pipes had been sounding, and at each beat my own heart throbbed. The wail of the tune, Bhairavi, seemed to intensify my pain at the approaching separation. My Mini was to be married to-night.

From early morning noise and bustle had pervaded the house. In the courtyard the canopy had to be slung on its bamboo poles; the chandeliers with their tinkling sound must be hung in each room and verandah. There was no end of hurry and excitement. I was sitting in my study, looking through the accounts, when some one entered, saluting respectfully, and stood before me. It was Rahmun the Cabuliwallah. At first I did not recognise him. He had no bag, nor the long hair, nor the same vigour that he used to have. But he smiled, and I knew him again.

"When did you come, Rahmun?" I asked him.

"Last evening," he said, "I was released from jail."

The words struck harsh upon my ears. I had never before talked with one who had wounded his fellow, and my heart shrank within itself, when I realised this, for I felt that the day would have been better-omened had he not turned up.

"There are ceremonies going on," I said, "and I am busy. Could you perhaps come another day?"

At once he turned to go; but as he reached the door he hesitated, and said: "May I not see the little one, sir, for a moment?" It was his belief that Mini was still the same. He had pictured her running to him as she used, calling "O Cabuliwallah! Cabuliwallah!" He had imagined too that they would laugh and talk together, just as of old. In fact, in memory of former days he had brought, carefully wrapped up in paper, a few almonds and raisins and grapes, obtained somehow from a countryman, for his own little fund was dispersed.

I said again: "There is a ceremony in the house, and you will not be able to see any one to-day."

The man's face fell. He looked wistfully at me for a moment, said "Good morning," and went out.

I felt a little sorry, and would have called him back,

but I found he was returning of his own accord. He came close up to me holding out his offerings and said: "I brought these few things, sir, for the little one. Will you give them to her?"

I took them and was going to pay him, but he caught my hand and said: "You are very kind, sir! Keep me in your recollection. Do not offer me money!—You have a little girl, I too have one like her in my own home. I think of her, and bring fruits to your child, not to make a profit for myself."

Saying this, he put his hand inside his big loose robe, and brought out a small and dirty piece of paper. With great care he unfolded this, and smoothed it out with both hands on my table. It bore the impression of a little hand. Not a photograph. Not a drawing. The impression of an ink-smeared hand laid flat on the paper. This touch of his own little daughter had been always on his heart, as he had come year after year to Calcutta, to sell his wares in the streets.

Tears came to my eyes. I forgot that he was a poor Cabuli fruit-seller, while I was—but no, what was I more than he? He also was a father.

That impression of the hand of his little *Pārbati* in her distant mountain home reminded me of my own little Mini.

I sent for Mini immediately from the inner apartment. Many difficulties were raised, but I would not listen. Clad in the red silk of her wedding-day, with the sandal paste on her forehead, and adorned as a young bride, Mini came, and stood bashfully before me.

The Cabuliwallah looked a little staggered at the apparition. He could not revive their old friendship. At last he smiled and said: "Little one, are you going to your father-in-law's house?"

But Mini now understood the meaning of the word "father-in-law," and she could not reply to him as of old. She flushed up at the question, and stood before him with her bride-like face turned down.

I remembered the day when the Cabuliwallah and my Mini had first met, and I felt sad. When she had gone, Rahmun heaved a deep sigh, and sat down on the floor. The idea had suddenly come to him that his daughter too must have grown in this long time, and that he would have to make friends with her anew. Assuredly he would not find her, as he used to know her. And besides, what might not have happened to her in these eight years?

The marriage-pipes sounded, and the mild autumn sun streamed round us. But Rahmun sat in the little Calcutta lane, and saw before him the barren mountains of Afghanistan.

I took out a bank-note, and gave it to him, saying: "Go back to your own daughter, Rahmun, in your own country, and may the happiness of your meeting bring good fortune to my child!"

Having made this present, I had to curtail some of

the festivities. I could not have the electric lights I had intended, nor the military band, and the ladies of the house were despondent at it. But to me the wedding feast was all the brighter for the thought that in a distant land a long-lost father met again with his only child.

Mashi

I

'MASHI!'*

'Try to sleep, Jotin, it is getting late.'

'Never mind if it is. I have not many days left. I was thinking that Mani should go to her father's house.—I forget where he is now.'

'Sitarampur.'

'Oh yes! Sitarampur. Send her there. She should not remain any longer near a sick man. She herself is not strong.'

'Just listen to him! How can she bear to leave you in this state?'

'Does she know what the doctors——?'

'But she can see for herself! The other day she cried her eyes out at the merest hint of having to go to her father's house.'

We must explain that in this statement there was a slight distortion of truth, to say the least of it. The actual talk with Mani was as follows:—

* The maternal aunt is addressed as Mashi.

'I suppose, my child, you have got some news from your father? I thought I saw your cousin Anath here.'

'Yes! Next Friday will be my little sister's *annaprashan** ceremony. So I'm thinking——'

'All right, my dear. Send her a gold necklace. It will please your mother.'

'I'm thinking of going myself. I've never seen my little sister, and I want to ever so much.'

'Whatever do you mean? You surely don't think of leaving Jotin alone? Haven't you heard what the doctor says about him?'

'But he said that just now there's no special cause for——'

'Even if he did, you can see his state.'

'This is the first girl after three brothers, and she's a great favourite.—I have heard that it's going to be a grand affair. If I don't go, mother will be very——'

'Yes, yes! I don't understand your mother. But I know very well that your father will be angry enough if you leave Jotin just now.'

'You'll have to write a line to him saying that there is no special cause for anxiety, and that even if I go, there will be no——'

'You're right there; it will certainly be no great loss if you do go. But remember, if I write to your father, I'll tell him plainly what is in my mind.'

* The *annaprashan* ceremony takes place when a child is first given rice. Usually it receives its name on that day.

'Then you needn't write. I shall ask my husband, and he will surely——'

'Look here, child, I've borne a good deal from you, but if you do that, I won't stand it for a moment. Your father knows you too well for you to deceive him.'

When Mashi had left her, Mani lay down on her bed in a bad temper.

Her neighbour and friend came and asked what was the matter.

'Look here! What a shame it is! Here's my only sister's *annaprashan* coming, and they don't want to let me go to it!'

'Why! Surely you're never thinking of going, are you, with your husband so ill?'

'I don't do anything for him, and I couldn't if I tried. It's so deadly dull in this house, that I tell you frankly I can't bear it.'

'You are a strange woman!'

'But I can't pretend, as you people do, and look glum lest any one should think ill of me.'

'Well, tell me your plan.'

'I must go. Nobody can prevent me.'

'Isss! What an imperious young woman you are!'

II

Hearing that Mani had wept at the mere thought of going to her father's house, Jotin was so excited that he sat up in bed. Pulling his pillow towards him, he leaned back, and said: 'Mashi, open this window a little, and take that lamp away.'

The still night stood silently at the window like a pilgrim of eternity; and the stars gazed in, witnesses through untold ages of countless death-scenes.

Jotin saw his Mani's face traced on the background of the dark night, and saw those two big dark eyes brimming over with tears, as it were for all eternity.

Mashi felt relieved when she saw him so quiet, thinking he was asleep.

Suddenly he started up, and said: 'Mashi, you all thought that Mani was too frivolous ever to be happy in our house. But you see now——'

'Yes, I see now, my Baba,* I was mistaken—but trial tests a person.'

'Mashi!'

'Do try to sleep, dear!'

'Let me think a little, let me talk. Don't be vexed, Mashi!'

'Very well.'

'Once, when I used to think I could not win Mani's heart, I bore it silently. But you——'

'No, dear, I won't allow you to say that; I also bore it.'

* Baba literally means Father, but is often used by elders as a term of endearment. In the same way 'Ma' is used.

'Our minds, you know, are not clods of earth which you can possess by merely picking up. I felt that Mani did not know her own mind, and that one day at some great shock——'

'Yes, Jotin, you are right.'

'Therefore I never took much notice of her waywardness.'

Mashi remained silent, suppressing a sigh. Not once, but often she had seen Jotin spending the night on the verandah wet with the splashing rain, yet not caring to go into his bedroom. Many a day he lay with a throbbing head, longing, she knew, that Mani would come and soothe his brow, while Mani was getting ready to go to the theatre. Yet when Mashi went to fan him, he sent her away petulantly. She alone knew what pain lay hidden in that distress. Again and again she had wanted to say to Jotin: 'Don't pay so much attention to that silly child, my dear; let her learn to want,—to cry for things.' But these things cannot be said, and are apt to be misunderstood. Jotin had in his heart a shrine set up to the goddess Woman, and there Mani had her throne. It was hard for him to imagine that his own fate was to be denied his share of the wine of love poured out by that divinity. Therefore the worship went on, the sacrifice was offered, and the hope of a boon never ceased.

Mashi imagined once more that Jotin was sleeping, when he cried out suddenly:

'I know you thought that I was not happy with Mani, and therefore you were angry with her. But, Mashi, happiness is like those stars. They don't cover all the darkness; there are gaps between. We make mistakes in life and we misunderstand, and yet there remain gaps through which truth shines. I do not know whence comes this gladness that fills my heart to-night.'

Mashi began gently to soothe Jotin's brow, her tears unseen in the dark.

'I was thinking, Mashi, she's so young! What will she do when I am——?'

'Young, Jotin? She's old enough. I too was young when I lost the idol of my life, only to find him in my heart for ever. Was that any loss, do you think? Besides, is happiness absolutely necessary?'

'Mashi, it seems as if just when Mani's heart shows signs of awakening I have to——'

'Don't you worry about that, Jotin. Isn't it enough if her heart awakes?'

Suddenly Jotin recollected the words of a village minstrel's song which he had heard long before:

O my heart! you woke not when the man of my heart
came to my door.
At the sound of his departing steps you woke up.
Oh, you woke up in the dark!

'Mashi, what is the time now?'

'About nine.'

'So early as that! Why, I thought it must be at least two or three o'clock. My midnight, you know, begins at sundown. But why did you want me to sleep, then?'

'Why, you know how late last night you kept awake talking; so to-day you must get to sleep early.'

'Is Mani asleep?'

'Oh no, she's busy making some soup for you.'

'You don't mean to say so, Mashi? Does she——?'

'Certainly! Why, she prepares all your food, the busy little woman.'

'I thought perhaps Mani could not——'

'It doesn't take long for a woman to learn such things. With the need it comes of itself.'

'The fish soup, that I had in the morning, had such a delicate flavour, I thought you had made it.'

'Dear me, no! Surely you don't think Mani would let me do anything for you? Why, she does all your washing herself. She knows you can't bear anything dirty about you. If only you could see your sitting-room, how spick and span she keeps it! If I were to let her haunt your sick-room, she would wear herself out. But that's what she really wants to do.'

'Is Mani's health, then——?'

'The doctors think she should not be allowed to visit the sick-room too often. She's too tender-hearted.'

'But, Mashi, how do you prevent her from coming?'

'Because she obeys me implicitly. But still I have constantly to be giving her news of you.'

The stars glistened in the sky like tear-drops. Jotin bowed his head in gratitude to his life that was about to depart, and when Death stretched out his right hand towards him through the darkness, he took it in perfect trust.

Jotin sighed, and, with a slight gesture of impatience, said:

'Mashi, if Mani is still awake, then, could I—if only for a——?'

'Very well! I'll go and call her.'

'I won't keep her long, only for five minutes. I have something particular to tell her.'

Mashi, sighing, went out to call Mani. Meanwhile Jotin's pulse began to beat fast. He knew too well that he had never been able to have an intimate talk with Mani. The two instruments were tuned differently and it was not easy to play them in unison. Again and again, Jotin had felt pangs of jealousy on hearing Mani chattering and laughing merrily with her girl companions. Jotin blamed only himself,—why couldn't he talk irrelevant trifles as they did? Not that he could not, for with his men friends he often chatted on all sorts of trivialities. But the small talk that suits men is not suitable for women. You can hold a philosophical discourse in monologue, ignoring your inattentive audience altogether, but small talk requires the co-operation of at least two. The bagpipes can be played singly, but there must be a pair of cymbals. How often in the evenings had Jotin, when sitting on the open verandah with Mani, made some strained attempts at conversation, only to feel the thread snap. And the very silence of the evening felt ashamed. Jotin was certain that Mani longed to get away. He had even wished earnestly that a third person would come. For talking is easy with three, when it is hard for two.

He began to think what he should say when Mani came. But such manufactured talk would not satisfy him. Jotin felt afraid that this five minutes of to-night would be wasted. Yet, for him, there were but few moments left for intimate talk.

III

'What's this, child, you're not going anywhere, are you?'

'Of course, I'm going to Sitarampur.'

'What do you mean? Who is going to take you?'

'Anath.'

'Not to-day, my child, some other day.'

'But the compartment has already been reserved.'

'What does that matter? That loss can easily be borne. Go to-morrow, early in the morning.'

'Mashi, I don't hold by your inauspicious days. What harm if I do go to-day?'

'Jotin wants to have a talk with you.'

'All right! there's still some time. I'll just go and see him.'

'But you mustn't say that you are going.'

'Very well, I won't tell him, but I shan't be able to stay long. To-morrow is my sister's *annaprashan,* and I must go to-day.'

'Oh, my child! I beg you to listen to me this once. Quiet your mind for a while and sit by him. Don't let him see your hurry.'

'What can I do? The train won't wait for me. Anath will be back in ten minutes. I can sit by him till then.'

'No, that won't do. I shall never let you go to him in that frame of mind. . . . Oh, you wretch! the man you are torturing is soon to leave this world; but I warn you, you will remember this day till the end of your days! That there is a God! that there is a God! you will some day understand!'

'Mashi, you mustn't curse me like that.'

'Oh, my darling boy! my darling! why do you go on living longer? There is no end to this sin, yet I cannot check it!'

Mashi after delaying a little returned to the sick-room, hoping by that time Jotin would be asleep. But Jotin moved in his bed when she entered. Mashi exclaimed:

'Just look what she has done!'

'What's happened? Hasn't Mani come? Why have you been so long, Mashi?'

'I found her weeping bitterly because she had allowed the milk for your soup to get burnt! I tried to console her, saying, "Why, there's more milk to be had!" But that she could be so careless about the preparation of *your* soup made her wild. With great trouble I managed to pacify her and put her to bed. So I haven't brought her to-day. Let her sleep it off.'

Though Jotin was pained when Mani didn't come, yet he felt a certain amount of relief. He had half feared that Mani's bodily presence would do violence to his heart's image of her. Such things had happened before in his life. And the gladness of the idea that Mani was miserable at burning *his* milk filled his heart to overflowing.

'Mashi!'

'What is it, Baba?'

'I feel quite certain that my days are drawing to a close. But I have no regrets. Don't grieve for me.'

'No, dear, I won't grieve. I don't believe that only life is good and not death.'

'Mashi, I tell you truly that death seems sweet.'

Jotin, gazing at the dark sky, felt that it was Mani herself who was coming to him in Death's guise. She had immortal youth and the stars were flowers of blessing, showered upon her dark tresses by the hand of the World-Mother. It seemed as if once more he had his first sight of his bride under the veil of darkness. The immense night became filled with the loving gaze of Mani's dark eyes. Mani, the bride of this house, the little girl, became transformed into a world-image,—her throne on the altar of the stars at the confluence of life and death. Jotin said to himself with clasped hands: 'At last the veil is raised, the covering is rent in this deep darkness. Ah, beautiful one! how often have you wrung my heart, but no longer shall you forsake me!'

IV

'I'm suffering, Mashi, but nothing like you imagine. It seems to me as if my pain were gradually separating itself from my life. Like a laden boat, it was so long being towed behind, but the rope has snapped, and now it floats away with all my burdens. Still I can see it, but it is no longer mine. . . . But, Mashi, I've not seen Mani even once for the last two days!'

'Jotin, let me give you another pillow.'

'It almost seems to me, Mashi, that Mani also has left me like that laden boat of sorrow which drifts away.'

'Just sip some pomegranate juice, dear! Your throat must be getting dry.'

'I wrote my will yesterday; did I show it to you? I can't recollect.'

'There's no need to show it to me, Jotin.'

'When mother died, I had nothing of my own. You fed me and brought me up. Therefore I was saying——'

'Nonsense, child! I had only this house and a little property. You earned the rest.'

'But this house——?'

'That's nothing. Why, you've added to it so much that it's difficult to find out where my house was!'

'I'm sure Mani's love for you is really——'

'Yes, yes! I know that, Jotin. Now you try to sleep.'

'Though I have bequeathed all my property to Mani, it is practically yours, Mashi. She will never disobey you.'

'Why are you worrying so much about that, dear?'

'All I have I owe to you. When you see my will don't think for a moment that——'

'What do you mean, Jotin? Do you think I shall mind for a moment because you give to Mani what belongs to you? Surely I'm not so mean as that?'

'But you also will have——'

'Look here, Jotin, I shall get angry with you. You want to console me with money!'

'Oh, Mashi, how I wish I could give you something better than money!'

'That you have done, Jotin!—more than enough. Haven't I had you to fill my lonely house? I must have won that great good-fortune in many previous births! You have given me so much that now, if my destiny's due is exhausted, I shall not complain. Yes, yes! Give away everything in Mani's name,—your house, your money, your carriage, and your land—such burdens are too heavy for me!'

'Of course I know you have lost your taste for the enjoyments of life, but Mani is so young that——'

'No! you mustn't say that. If you want to leave her your property, it is all right, but as for enjoyment——'

'What harm if she does enjoy herself, Mashi?'

'No, no, it will be impossible. Her throat will become parched, and it will be dust and ashes to her.'

Jotin remained silent. He could not decide whether it was true or not, and whether it was a matter of regret or otherwise, that the world would become distasteful to Mani for want of him. The stars seemed to whisper in his heart:

'Indeed it is true. We have been watching for thousands of years, and know that all these great preparations for enjoyment are but vanity.'

Jotin sighed and said: 'We cannot leave behind us what is really worth giving.'

'It's no trifle you are giving, dearest. I only pray she may have the power to know the value of what is given her.'

'Give me a little more of that pomegranate juice, Mashi, I'm thirsty. Did Mani come to me yesterday, I wonder?'

'Yes, she came, but you were asleep. She sat by your head, fanning you for a long time, and then went away to get your clothes washed.'

'How wonderful! I believe I was dreaming that very moment that Mani was trying to enter my room. The door was slightly open, and she was pushing against it, but it wouldn't open. But, Mashi, you're going too far,—you ought to let her see that I am dying; otherwise my death will be a terrible shock to her.'

'Baba, let me put this shawl over your feet; they are getting cold.'

'No, Mashi, I can't bear anything over me like that.'

'Do you know, Jotin, Mani made this shawl for you? When she ought to have been asleep, she was busy at it. It was finished only yesterday.'

Jotin took the shawl, and touched it tenderly with his hands. It seemed to him that the softness of the wool was Mani's own. Her loving thoughts had been woven night after night with its threads. It was not made merely of wool, but also of her touch. Therefore, when Mashi drew that shawl over his feet, it seemed as if, night after night, Mani had been caressing his tired limbs.

'But, Mashi, I thought Mani didn't know how to knit,—at any rate she never liked it.'

'It doesn't take long to learn a thing. Of course I had to teach her. Then there are a good many mistakes in it.'

'Let there be mistakes; we're not going to send it to the Paris Exhibition. It will keep my feet warm in spite of its mistakes.'

Jotin's mind began to picture Mani at her task, blundering and struggling, and yet patiently going on night after night. How sweetly pathetic it was! And again he went over the shawl with his caressing fingers.

'Mashi, is the doctor downstairs?'

'Yes, he will stay here to-night.'

'But tell him it is useless for him to give me a sleeping draught. It doesn't bring me real rest and only adds to my pain. Let me remain properly awake. Do you know, Mashi, that my wedding took place on the night of the full moon in the month of *Baisakh*? To-morrow will be that day, and the stars of that very night will be shining in the sky. Mani perhaps has forgotten. I want to remind her of it to-day; just call her to me for a minute or two. . . . Why do you keep silent? I suppose the doctor has told you I am so weak that any excitement will——but I tell you truly, Mashi, to-night, if I can have only a few minutes' talk with her, there will be no need for any sleeping draughts. Mashi, don't cry like that! I am quite well. To-day my heart is full as it has never been in my life before. That's why I want to see Mani. No, no, Mashi, I can't bear to see you crying! You have been so quiet all these last days. Why are you so troubled to-night?'

'Oh, Jotin, I thought that I had exhausted all my tears, but I find there are plenty left. I can't bear it any longer.'

'Call Mani. I'll remind her of our wedding night, so that to-morrow she may——'

'I'm going, dear. Shombhu will wait at the door. If you want anything, call him.'

Mashi went to Mani's bedroom and sat down on the floor crying,—'Oh come, come once, you heartless wretch! Keep his last request who has given you his all! Don't kill him who is already dying!'

Jotin hearing the sound of footsteps started up, saying, 'Mani!'

'I am Shombhu. Did you call me?'

'Ask your mistress to come?'

'Ask whom?'

'Your mistress.'

'She has not yet returned.'

'Returned? From where?'

'From Sitarampur.'

'When did she go?'

'Three days ago.'

For a moment Jotin felt numb all over, and his head began to swim. He slipped down from the pillows, on which he was reclining, and kicked off the woollen shawl that was over his feet.

When Mashi came back after a long time, Jotin did not mention Mani's name, and Mashi thought he had forgotten all about her.

Suddenly Jotin cried out: 'Mashi, did I tell you about the dream I had the other night?'

'Which dream?'

'That in which Mani was pushing the door, and the door wouldn't open more than an inch. She stood outside unable to enter. Now I know that Mani has to stand outside my door till the last.'

Mashi kept silent. She realised that the heaven she had been building for Jotin out of falsehood had toppled down at last. If sorrow comes, it is best to acknowledge it.—When God strikes, we cannot avoid the blow.

'Mashi, the love I have got from you will last through all my births. I have filled this life with it to carry it with me. In the next birth, I am sure you will be born as my daughter, and I shall tend you with all my love.'

'What are you saying, Jotin? Do you mean to say I shall be born again as a woman? Why can't you pray that I should come to your arms as a son?'

'No, no, not a son! You will come to my house in that wonderful beauty which you had when you were young. I can even imagine how I shall dress you.'

'Don't talk so much, Jotin, but try to sleep.'

'I shall name you "Lakshmi."'

'But that is an old-fashioned name, Jotin!'

'Yes, but you are my old-fashioned Mashi. Come to my house again with those beautiful old-fashioned manners.'

'I can't wish that I should come and burden your home with the misfortune of a girl-child!'

'Mashi, you think me weak, and are wanting to save me all trouble.'

'My child, I am a woman, so I have my weakness. Therefore I have tried all my life to save you from all sorts of trouble,—only to fail.'

'Mashi, I have not had time in this life to apply the lessons I have learnt. But they will keep for my next birth. I shall show then what a man is able to do. I have learnt how false it is always to be looking after oneself.'

'Whatever you may say, darling, you have never grasped anything for yourself, but given everything to others.'

'Mashi, I can boast of one thing at any rate. I have never been a tyrant in my happiness, or tried to enforce my claims by violence. Because lies could not content me, I have had to wait long. Perhaps truth will be kind to me at last.—Who is that, Mashi, who is that?'

'Where? There's no one there, Jotin!'

'Mashi, just go and see in the other room. I thought I——'

'No, dear! I don't see anybody.'

'But it seemed quite clear to me that——'

'No, Jotin, it's nothing. So keep quiet! The doctor is coming now.'

When the doctor entered, he said:

'Look here, you mustn't stay near the patient so much, you excite him. You go to bed, and my assistant will remain with him.'

'No, Mashi, I can't let you go.'

'All right, Baba! I will sit quietly in that corner.'

'No, no! you must sit by my side. I can't let go your hand, not till the very end. I have been made by your hand, and only from your hand shall God take me.'

'All right,' said the doctor, 'you can remain there. But, Jotin Babu, you must not talk to her. It's time for you to take your medicine.'

'Time for my medicine? Nonsense! The time for that is over. To give medicine now is merely to deceive; besides I am not afraid to die. Mashi, Death is busy with his physic; why do you add another nuisance in the shape of a doctor? Send him away, send him away! It is you alone I need now! No one else, none whatever! No more falsehood!'

'I protest, as a doctor, this excitement is doing you harm.'

'Then go, doctor, don't excite me any more!—Mashi, has he gone? . . . That's good! Now come and take my head in your lap.'

'All right, dear! Now, Baba, try to sleep!'

'No, Mashi, don't ask me to sleep. If I sleep, I shall never wake. I still need to keep awake a little longer. Don't you hear a sound? Somebody is coming.'

V

'Jotin dear, just open your eyes a little. She has come. Look once and see!'

'Who has come? A dream?'

'Not a dream, darling! Mani has come with her father.'

'Who are you?'

'Can't you see? This is your Mani!'

'Mani? Has that door opened?'

'Yes, Baba, it is wide open.'

'No, Mashi, not that shawl! not *that* shawl! That shawl is a fraud!'

'It is not a shawl, Jotin! It is our Mani, who has flung herself on your feet. Put your hand on her head and bless her. Don't cry like that, Mani! There will be time enough for that. Keep quiet now for a little.'

The Skeleton

In the room next to the one in which we boys used to sleep, there hung a human skeleton. In the night it would rattle in the breeze which played about its bones. In the day these bones were rattled by us. We were taking lessons in osteology from a student in the Campbell Medical School, for our guardians were determined to make us masters of all the sciences. How far they succeeded we need not tell those who know us; and it is better hidden from those who do not.

Many years have passed since then. In the meantime the skeleton has vanished from the room, and the science of osteology from our brains, leaving no trace behind.

The other day, our house was crowded with guests, and I had to pass the night in the same old room. In these now unfamiliar surroundings, sleep refused to come, and, as I tossed from side to side, I heard all the hours of the night chimed, one after another, by the church clock near by. At length the lamp in the corner of the room, after some minutes of choking and spluttering, went out altogether. One or two bereavements had recently happened in the family, so the going out of the lamp naturally led me to thoughts of death. In the great arena of nature, I thought, the light of a lamp losing itself in eternal darkness, and the going out of the light of our little human lives, by day or by night, were much the same thing.

My train of thought recalled to my mind the skeleton. While I was trying to imagine what the body which had clothed it could have been like, it suddenly seemed to me that something was walking round and round my bed, groping along the walls of the room. I could hear its rapid breathing. It seemed as if it was searching for something which it could not find, and pacing round the room with ever-hastier steps. I felt quite sure that this was a mere fancy of my sleepless, excited brain; and that the throbbing of the veins in my temples was really the sound which seemed like running footsteps. Nevertheless, a cold shiver ran all over me. To help to get rid of this hallucination, I called out aloud: 'Who is there?' The footsteps seemed to stop at my bedside, and the reply came: 'It is I. I have come to look for that skeleton of mine.'

It seemed absurd to show any fear before the creature of my own imagination; so, clutching my pillow a little more tightly, I said in a casual sort of way: 'A nice business for this time of night! Of what use will that skeleton be to you now?'

The reply seemed to come almost from my mosquito-curtain itself. 'What a question! In that skeleton were the bones that encircled my heart; the youthful charm of my six-and-twenty years bloomed about it. Should I not desire to see it once more?'

'Of course,' said I, 'a perfectly reasonable desire. Well, go on with your search, while I try to get a little sleep.'

Said the voice: 'But I fancy you are lonely. All right; I'll sit down a while, and we will have a little chat. Years ago I used to sit by men and talk to them. But during the last thirty-five years I have only moaned in the wind in the burning-places of the dead. I would talk once more with a man as in the old times.'

I felt that some one sat down just near my curtain. Resigning myself to the situation, I replied with as much cordiality as I could summon: 'That will be very nice indeed. Let us talk of something cheerful.'

'The funniest thing I can think of is my own life-story. Let me tell you that.'

The church clock chimed the hour of two.

'When I was in the land of the living, and young, I feared one thing like death itself, and that was my husband. My feelings can be likened only to those of a fish caught with a hook. For it was as if a stranger had snatched me away with the sharpest of hooks from the peaceful calm of my childhood's home—and from him I had no means of escape. My husband died two months after my marriage, and my friends and relations moaned pathetically on my behalf. My husband's father, after scrutinising my face with great care, said to my mother-in-law: "Do you not see, she has the evil eye?"—Well, are you listening? I hope you are enjoying the story?'

'Very much indeed!' said I. 'The beginning is extremely humorous.'

'Let me proceed then. I came back to my father's house in great glee. People tried to conceal it from me, but I knew well that I was endowed with a rare and radiant beauty. What is your opinion?'

'Very likely,' I murmured. 'But you must remember that I never saw you.'

'What! Not seen me? What about that skeleton of mine? Ha! ha! ha! Never mind. I was only joking. How can I ever make you believe that those two cavernous hollows contained the brightest of dark, languishing eyes? And that the smile which was revealed by those ruby lips had no resemblance whatever to the grinning teeth which you used to see? The mere attempt to convey to you some idea of the grace, the charm, the soft, firm, dimpled curves, which in the fulness of youth were growing and blossoming over those dry old bones makes me smile; it also makes me angry. The most eminent doctors of my time could not have dreamed of the bones of that body of mine as materials for teaching osteology. Do you know, one young doctor that I knew of, actually compared me to a golden *champak* blossom. It meant that to him the rest of humankind was fit only to illustrate the science of physiology, that I was a flower of beauty. Does any one think of the skeleton of a *champak* flower?

'When I walked, I felt that, like a diamond scattering splendour, my every movement set waves of beauty radiating on every side. I used to spend hours gazing on my hands—hands which could gracefully have reined the liveliest of male creatures.

'But that stark and staring old skeleton of mine has borne false-witness to you against me, while I was unable to refute the shameless libel. That is why of all men I hate you most! I feel I would like once for all to banish sleep from your eyes with a vision of that warm rosy loveliness of mine, to sweep out with it all the wretched osteological stuff of which your brain is full.'

'I could have sworn by your body,' cried I, 'if you had it still, that no vestige of osteology has remained in my head, and that the only thing that it is now full of is a radiant vision of perfect loveliness, glowing against the black background of night. I cannot say more than that.'

'I had no girl-companions,' went on the voice. 'My only brother had made up his mind not to marry. In the zenana I was alone. Alone I used to sit in the garden under the shade of the trees, and dream that the whole world was in love with me; that the stars with sleepless gaze were drinking in my beauty; that the wind was languishing in sighs as on some pretext or other it brushed past me; and that the lawn on which my feet rested, had it been conscious, would have lost consciousness again at their touch. It seemed to me that all the young men in the world were as blades of grass at my feet; and my heart, I know not why, used to grow sad.

'When my brother's friend, Shekhar, had passed out of the Medical College, he became our family doctor. I had already often seen him from behind a curtain. My brother was a strange man, and did not care to look on the world with open eyes. It was not empty enough for his taste; so he gradually moved away from it, until he was quite lost in an obscure corner. Shekhar was his one friend, so he was the only young man I could ever get to see. And when I held my evening court in my garden, then the host of imaginary young men whom I had at my feet were each one a Shekhar.—Are you listening? What are you thinking of?'

I sighed as I replied: 'I was wishing I was Shekhar!'

'Wait a bit. Hear the whole story first. One day, in the rains, I was feverish. The doctor came to see me. That was our first meeting. I was reclining opposite the window, so that the blush of the evening sky might temper the pallor of my complexion. When the doctor, coming in, looked up into my face, I put myself into his place, and gazed at myself in imagination. I saw in the glorious evening light that delicate wan face laid like a drooping flower against the soft white pillow, with the unrestrained curls playing over the forehead, and the bashfully lowered eyelids casting a pathetic shade over the whole countenance.

'The doctor, in a tone bashfully low, asked my brother: "Might I feel her pulse?"

'I put out a tired, well-rounded wrist from beneath the coverlet. "Ah!" thought I, as I looked on it, "if only there had been a sapphire bracelet." I have never before seen a doctor so awkward about feeling a patient's pulse. His fingers trembled as they felt my wrist. He measured the heat of my fever, I gauged the pulse of his heart.—Don't you believe me?'

'Very easily,' said I; 'the human heart-beat tells its tale.'

'After I had been taken ill and restored to health several times, I found that the number of the courtiers who attended my imaginary evening reception began to dwindle till they were reduced to only one! And at last in my little world there remained only one doctor and one patient.

'In these evenings I used to dress myself secretly in a canary-coloured *sari*; twine about the braided knot into which I did my hair a garland of white jasmine blossoms; and with a little mirror in my hand betake myself to my usual seat under the trees.

'Well! Are you perhaps thinking that the sight of one's own beauty would soon grow wearisome? Ah no! for I did not see myself with my own eyes. I was then one and also two. I used to see myself as though I were the doctor; I gazed, I was charmed, I fell madly in love. But, in spite of all the caresses I lavished on myself, a sigh would wander about my heart, moaning like the evening breeze.

'Anyhow, from that time I was never alone. When I walked I watched with downcast eyes the play of my dainty little toes on the earth, and wondered what the doctor would have felt had he been there to see. At mid-day the sky would be filled with the glare of the sun, without a sound, save now and then the distant cry of a passing kite. Outside our garden-walls the hawker would pass with his musical cry of "Bangles for sale, crystal bangles." And I, spreading a snow-white sheet on the lawn, would lie on it with my head on my arm. With studied carelessness the other arm would rest lightly on the soft sheet, and I would imagine to myself that some one had caught sight of the wonderful pose of my hand, that some one had clasped it in both of his and imprinted a kiss on its rosy palm, and was slowly walking away.—What if I ended the story here? How would it do?'

'Not half a bad ending,' I replied thoughtfully. 'It would no doubt remain a little incomplete, but I could easily spend the rest of the night putting in the finishing touches.'

'But that would make the story too serious. Where would the laugh come in? Where would be the skeleton with its grinning teeth?

'So let me go on. As soon as the doctor had got a little practice, he took a room on the ground-floor of our house for a consulting-chamber. I used then sometimes to ask him jokingly about medicines and poisons, and how much of this drug or that would kill a man. The subject was congenial and he would wax eloquent. These talks familiarised me with the idea of death; and so love and death were the only two things that filled my little world. My story is now nearly ended—there is not much left.'

'Not much of the night is left either,' I muttered.

'After a time I noticed that the doctor had grown strangely absent-minded, and it seemed as if he were ashamed of something which he was trying to keep from me. One day he came in, somewhat smartly dressed, and borrowed my brother's carriage for the evening.

'My curiosity became too much for me, and I went up to my brother for information. After some talk beside the point, I at last asked him: "By the way, Dada,* where is the doctor going this evening in your carriage?"

'My brother briefly replied: "To his death."

'"Oh, do tell me," I importuned. "Where is he really going?"

'"To be married," he said, a little more explicitly.

'"Oh, indeed!" said I, as I laughed long and loudly.

'I gradually learnt that the bride was an heiress, who would bring the doctor a large sum of money. But why did he insult me by hiding all this from me? Had I ever

* Elder brother.

begged and prayed him not to marry, because it would break my heart? Men are not to be trusted. I have known only one man in all my life, and in a moment I made this discovery.

'When the doctor came in after his work and was ready to start, I said to him, rippling with laughter the while: "Well, doctor, so you are to be married to-night?"

'My gaiety not only made the doctor lose countenance; it thoroughly irritated him.

'"How is it," I went on, "that there is no illumination, no band of music?"

'With a sigh he replied: "Is marriage then such a joyful occasion?"

'I burst out into renewed laughter. "No, no," said I, "this will never do. Who ever heard of a wedding without lights and music?"

'I bothered my brother about it so much that he at once ordered all the trappings of a gay wedding.

'All the time I kept on gaily talking of the bride, of what would happen, of what I would do when the bride came home. "And, doctor," I asked, "will you still go on feeling pulses?" Ha! ha! ha! Though the inner workings of people's, especially men's, minds are not visible, still I can take my oath that these words were piercing the doctor's bosom like deadly darts.

'The marriage was to be celebrated late at night. Before starting, the doctor and my brother were having a glass of wine together on the terrace, as was their daily habit. The moon had just risen.

'I went up smiling, and said: "Have you forgotten your wedding, doctor? It is time to start."

'I must here tell you one little thing. I had meanwhile gone down to the dispensary and got a little powder, which at a convenient opportunity I had dropped unobserved into the doctor's glass.

'The doctor, draining his glass at a gulp, in a voice thick with emotion, and with a look that pierced me to the heart, said: "Then I must go."

'The music struck up. I went into my room and dressed myself in my bridal-robes of silk and gold. I took out my jewellery and ornaments from the safe and put them all on; I put the red mark of wifehood on the parting in my hair. And then under the tree in the garden I prepared my bed.

'It was a beautiful night. The gentle south wind was kissing away the weariness of the world. The scent of jasmine and *bela* filled the garden with rejoicing.

'When the sound of the music began to grow fainter and fainter; the light of the moon to get dimmer and dimmer; the world with its lifelong associations of home and kin to fade away from my perceptions like some illusion;—then I closed my eyes, and smiled.

'I fancied that when people came and found me they would see that smile of mine lingering on my lips like a trace of rose-coloured wine, that when I thus slowly entered my eternal bridal-chamber I should carry with me this smile, illuminating my face. But alas for the bridal-chamber! Alas for the bridal-robes of silk and gold! When I woke at the sound of a rattling within me, I found three urchins learning osteology from my skeleton. Where in my bosom my joys and griefs used to throb, and the petals of youth to open one by one, there the master with his pointer was busy naming my bones. And as to that last smile, which I had so carefully rehearsed, did you see any sign of that?

'Well, well, how did you like the story?'

'It has been delightful,' said I.

At this point the first crow began to caw. Are you there?' I asked. There was no reply.

The morning light entered the room.

The Postmaster

The postmaster first took up his duties in the village of Ulapur. Though the village was a small one, there was an indigo factory near by, and the proprietor, an Englishman, had managed to get a post office established.

Our postmaster belonged to Calcutta. He felt like a fish out of water in this remote village. His office and living-room were in a dark thatched shed, not far from a green, slimy pond, surrounded on all sides by a dense growth.

The men employed in the indigo factory had no leisure; moreover, they were hardly desirable companions for decent folk. Nor is a Calcutta boy an adept in the art of associating with others. Among strangers he appears either proud or ill at ease. At any rate, the postmaster had but little company; nor had he much to do.

At times he tried his hand at writing a verse or two. That the movement of the leaves and the clouds of the sky were enough to fill life with joy—such were the sentiments to which he sought to give expression. But God knows that the poor fellow would have felt it as the gift of a new life, if some genie of the *Arabian Nights* had in one night swept away the trees, leaves and all, and replaced them with a macadamised road, hiding the clouds from view with rows of tall houses.

The postmaster's salary was small. He had to cook his own meals, which he used to share with Ratan, an orphan girl of the village, who did odd jobs for him.

When in the evening the smoke began to curl up from the village cow-sheds,* and the cicalas chirped in every bush; when the faquirs of the Baul sect sang their shrill songs in their daily meeting-place, when any poet, who had attempted to watch the movement of the leaves in the dense bamboo thickets, would have felt a ghostly shiver run down his back, the postmaster would light his little lamp, and call out 'Ratan.'

Ratan would sit outside waiting for this call, and, instead of coming in at once, would reply: 'Did you call me, sir?'

'What are you doing?' the postmaster would ask.

'I must be going to light the kitchen fire,' would be the answer.

And the postmaster would say: 'Oh, let the kitchen fire be for awhile; light me my pipe first.'

At last Ratan would enter, with puffed-out cheeks, vigorously blowing into a flame a live coal to light the tobacco. This would give the postmaster an opportunity of conversing. 'Well, Ratan,' perhaps he would begin, 'do

* Smoky fires are lit in the cow-sheds to drive off mosquitoes.

you remember anything of your mother?' That was a fertile subject. Ratan partly remembered, and partly didn't. Her father had been fonder of her than her mother; him she recollected more vividly. He used to come home in the evening after his work, and one or two evenings stood out more clearly than others, like pictures in her memory. Ratan would squat on the floor near the postmaster's feet, as memories crowded in upon her. She called to mind a little brother that she had—and how on some bygone cloudy day she had played at fishing with him on the edge of the pond, with a twig for a make-believe fishing-rod. Such little incidents would drive out greater events from her mind. Thus, as they talked, it would often get very late, and the postmaster would feel too lazy to do any cooking at all. Ratan would then hastily light the fire, and toast some unleavened bread, which, with the cold remnants of the morning meal, was enough for their supper.

On some evenings, seated at his desk in the corner of the big empty shed, the postmaster too would call up memories of his own home, of his mother and his sister, of those for whom in his exile his heart was sad,—memories which were always haunting him, but which he could not talk about with the men of the factory, though he found himself naturally recalling them aloud in the presence of the simple little girl. And so it came about that the girl would allude to his people as mother, brother, and sister,* as if she had known them all her life. In fact, she had a complete picture of each one of them painted in her little heart.

One noon, during a break in the rains, there was a cool soft breeze blowing; the smell of the damp grass and leaves in the hot sun felt like the warm breathing of the tired earth on one's body. A persistent bird went on all the afternoon repeating the burden of its one complaint in Nature's audience chamber.

The postmaster had nothing to do. The shimmer of the freshly washed leaves, and the banked-up remnants of the retreating rain-clouds were sights to see; and the postmaster was watching them, and thinking to himself: 'Oh, if only some kindred soul were near—just one loving human being whom I could hold near my heart!' This was exactly, he went on to think, what that bird was trying to say, and it was the same feeling which the murmuring leaves were striving to express. But no one knows, or would believe, that such an idea might also take possession of an ill-paid village postmaster in the deep, silent midday interval of his work.

The postmaster sighed, and called out 'Ratan.' Ratan was then sprawling beneath the guava-tree, busily engaged in eating unripe guavas. At the voice of her master, she ran up breathlessly, saying: 'Were you calling

* Family servants call the master and mistress father and mother and the children elder brothers and sisters.

me, Dada?'* 'I was thinking,' said the postmaster, 'of teaching you to read,' and then for the rest of the afternoon he taught her the alphabet.

Thus, in a very short time, Ratan had got as far as the double consonants.

It seemed as though the showers of the season would never end. Canals, ditches, and hollows were all overflowing with water. Day and night the patter of rain was heard, and the croaking of frogs. The village roads became impassable, and marketing had to be done in punts.

One heavily clouded morning, the postmaster's little pupil had been long waiting outside the door for her call, but, not hearing it as usual, she took up her dog-eared book, and slowly entered the room. She found her master stretched out on his pallet, and, thinking he was resting, she was about to retire on tip-toe, when she suddenly heard her name—'Ratan!' She turned at once and asked: 'Were you sleeping, Dada?' The postmaster in a plaintive voice said: 'I am not well. Feel my head; is it very hot?'

In the loneliness of his exile, and in the gloom of the rains, his ailing body needed a little tender nursing. He longed to remember the touch on the forehead of soft hands with tinkling bracelets, to imagine the presence of loving womanhood, the nearness of mother and

* Dada = elder brother.

sister. And the exile was not disappointed. Ratan ceased to be a little girl. She at once stepped into the post of mother, called in the village doctor, gave the patient his pills at the proper intervals, sat up all night by his pillow, cooked his gruel for him, and every now and then asked: 'Are you feeling a little better, Dada?'

It was some time before the postmaster, with weakened body, was able to leave his sick-bed. 'No more of this,' said he with decision. 'I must get a transfer.' He at once wrote off to Calcutta an application for a transfer, on the ground of the unhealthiness of the place.

Relieved from her duties as nurse, Ratan again took up her old place outside the door. But she no longer heard the same old call. She would sometimes peep inside furtively to find the postmaster sitting on his chair, or stretched on his pallet, and staring absent-mindedly into the air. While Ratan was awaiting her call, the postmaster was awaiting a reply to his application. The girl read her old lessons over and over again—her great fear was lest, when the call came, she might be found wanting in the double consonants. At last, after a week, the call did come one evening. With an overflowing heart Ratan rushed into the room with her—'Were you calling me, Dada?'

The postmaster said: 'I am going away tomorrow, Ratan.'

'Where are you going, Dada?'

'I am going home.'

'When will you come back?'

'I am not coming back.'

Ratan asked no other question. The postmaster, of his own accord, went on to tell her that his application for a transfer had been rejected, so he had resigned his post, and was going home.

For a long time neither of them spoke another word. The lamp went on dimly burning, and from a leak in one corner of the thatch water dripped steadily into an earthen vessel on the floor beneath it.

After a while Ratan rose, and went off to the kitchen to prepare the meal; but she was not so quick about it as on other days. Many new things to think of had entered her little brain. When the postmaster had finished his supper, the girl suddenly asked him: 'Dada, will you take me to your home?'

The postmaster laughed. 'What an idea!' said he; but he did not think it necessary to explain to the girl wherein lay the absurdity.

That whole night, in her waking and in her dreams, the postmaster's laughing reply haunted her—'What an idea!'

On getting up in the morning, the postmaster found his bath ready. He had stuck to his Calcutta habit of bathing in water drawn and kept in pitchers, instead of taking a plunge in the river as was the custom of the village. For some reason or other, the girl could not ask him about the time of his departure, so she had fetched the water from the river long before sunrise, that it should be ready as early as he might want it. After the bath came a call for Ratan. She entered noiselessly, and looked silently into her master's face for orders. The master said: 'You need not be anxious about my going away, Ratan; I shall tell my successor to look after you.' These words were kindly meant, no doubt: but inscrutable are the ways of a woman's heart!

Ratan had borne many a scolding from her master without complaint, but these kind words she could not bear. She burst out weeping, and said: 'No, no, you need not tell anybody anything at all about me; I don't want to stay on here.'

The postmaster was dumbfounded. He had never seen Ratan like this before.

The new incumbent duly arrived, and the postmaster, having given over charge, prepared to depart. Just before starting he called Ratan, and said: 'Here is something for you; I hope it will keep you for some little time.' He brought out from his pocket the whole of his month's salary, retaining only a trifle for his travelling expenses. Then Ratan fell at his feet and cried: 'Oh, Dada, I pray you, don't give me anything, don't in any way trouble about me,' and then she ran away out of sight.

The postmaster heaved a sigh, took up his carpet bag, put his umbrella over his shoulder, and, accompanied by a man carrying his many-coloured tin trunk, he slowly made for the boat.

When he got in and the boat was under way, and the rain-swollen river, like a stream of tears welling up from the earth, swirled and sobbed at her bows, then he felt a sort of pain at heart; the grief-stricken face of a village girl seemed to represent for him the great unspoken pervading grief of Mother Earth herself. At one time he had an impulse to go back, and bring away along with him that lonesome waif, forsaken of the world. But the wind had just filled the sails, the boat had got well into the middle of the turbulent current, and already the village was left behind, and its outlying burning-ground came in sight.

So the traveller, borne on the breast of the swift-flowing river, consoled himself with philosophical reflections on the numberless meetings and partings going on in the world—on death, the great parting, from which none returns.

But Ratan had no philosophy. She was wandering about the post office in a flood of tears. It may be that she had still a lurking hope in some corner of her heart that her Dada would return, and that is why she could not tear herself away. Alas for the foolish human heart!

MACMILLAN COLLECTOR'S LIBRARY

All the books in this series:

A Carnival Jangle by Alice Dunbar Nelson

A Little Cloud by James Joyce

An Unwritten Novel by Virginia Woolf

The Home-Coming by Rabindranath Tagore

Jack and Alice by Jane Austen

The Curious Case of Benjamin Button
by F. Scott Fitzgerald

The Daughters of the Late Colonel
by Katherine Mansfield

The Murders in the Rue Morgue
by Edgar Allan Poe

The Nightingale and the Rose by Oscar Wilde

The Speckled Band by Arthur Conan Doyle